NICK JR. BLUE'S ROOM

Alphabet Power

adapted by Alison Inches
based on the teleplay by Alice Wilder

Simon Spotlight/Nick Jr.
New York   London   Toronto   Sydney

Based on the TV series *Blue's Clues*® created by Traci Paige Johnson,
Todd Kessler, and Angela C. Santomero as seen on Nick Jr.®
Photos by Joan Marcus and Ken Karp Photography.

SIMON SPOTLIGHT
An imprint of Simon & Schuster Children's Publishing Division
1230 Avenue of the Americas, New York, New York 10020
Copyright © 2005 Viacom International Inc. All rights reserved.
NICK JR., *Blue's Clues, Blue's Room*, and all related titles, logos,
and characters are trademarks of Viacom International Inc. Created by Traci Paige Johnson,
Todd Kessler, and Angela C. Santomero.
All rights reserved, including the right of reproduction in whole or in part in any form.
SIMON SPOTLIGHT and colophon are registered trademarks of Simon & Schuster, Inc.
Manufactured in the United States of America
10 9 8 7 6 5 4 3
ISBN-13: 978-1-4169-0709-1
ISBN-10: 1-4169-0709-2

Hi, YOU! Do you want to play? I love having playdates with you in B-B-B-Blue's Room!

Let's spin the Playdate Spinner to see what we'll play today!

Will you blow on the spinner with me? Ready? Let's blow!

It landed on ABCs! Hooray!

What do you think we can do in an ABC playdate?

The alphabet came over to play! Come on in, Alphabet. There's so much we can do with *alphabet power!*

Hey, I know a song about the alphabet. Do you want to sing it with me?

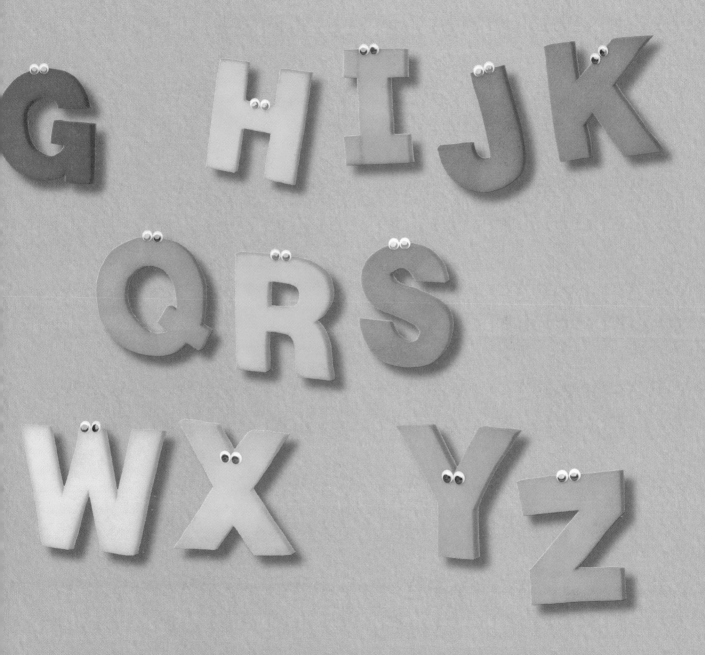

Now we know our ABCs. The best part is you sang with me!

Oooooh! Polka Dots has a special Polka Dots Puzzle Surprise word for us! I wonder what we're going to spell. Our first puzzle piece is the letter *R*. *R* is for Roar E. Saurus and his roaring! What else begins with the letter *R*?

Doodleboard is going to doodle a picture of something that starts with the letter D—just like his name, Doodle. Then we'll guess what it is. Ready?

Doodle, doodle, doodle. Doodle, doodle, doodle. Doodle, doodle, doodle. . . . Guess!

What do you think it is?

It's a dog! Dog starts with the letter D.
Doodleboard has alphabet power too!

Look! Our second Polka Dots puzzle piece is the letter E. Polka Dots says E is for elephant.

There goes our friend Frederica! Fred's chasing the alphabet because she wants to be a writer. Do you know what the word "writer" means?

Let's ask . . . DICTIONARY! Dictionary says that a writer is a person who writes down words on paper that tell a story.

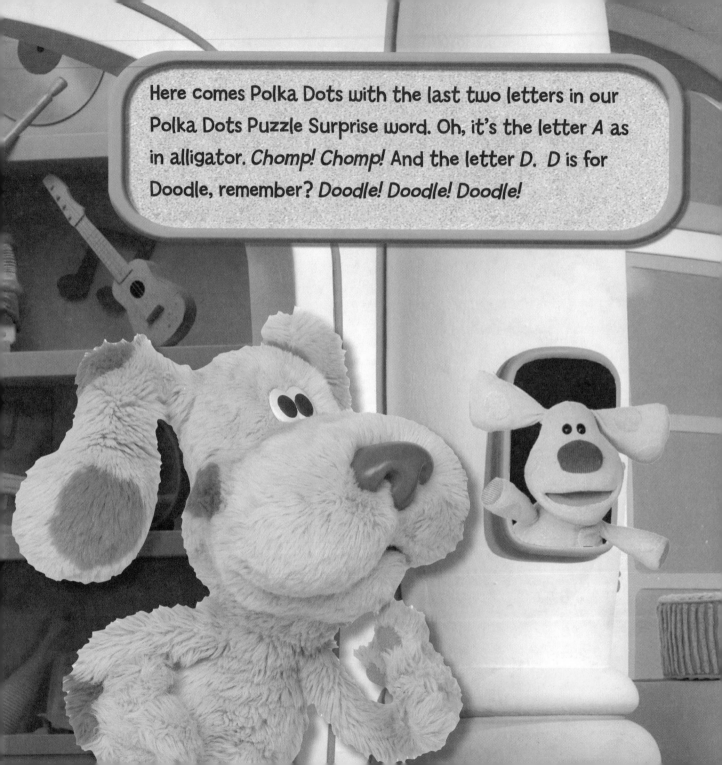

Here comes Polka Dots with the last two letters in our Polka Dots Puzzle Surprise word. Oh, it's the letter *A* as in alligator. *Chomp! Chomp!* And the letter *D*. *D* is for Doodle, remember? *Doodle! Doodle! Doodle!*

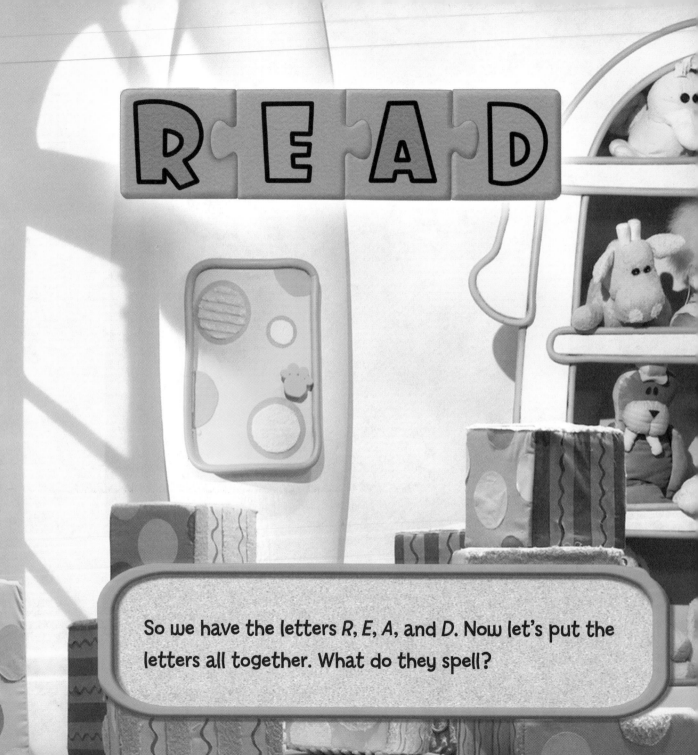

So we have the letters *R, E, A,* and *D.* Now let's put the letters all together. What do they spell?

R . . . E . . . A . . . D. That spells *read*. Wow! We have the power of the alphabet . . . to read. Do you have a favorite book you like to read?